DATE DUE

NOV 4 1994			

E
HEI

4509

Heide, Florence Parry
Look! Look!   X28676

FLORENCE PARRY HEIDE

LOOK! LOOK! A STORY BOOK

Illustrated by
Carol Nicklaus

THE McCALL PUBLISHING COMPANY • NEW YORK

To Paul Mathews,
who drew me a cat on a mat

LOOK! LOOK! A STORY BOOK
Copyright© 1971 by Florence Parry Heide
Illustrations copyright© 1971 by Plasencia Design
Associates, Inc., New York
All rights reserved.

Published simultaneously in Canada by
Doubleday Canada, Ltd., Toronto

Library of Congress Catalog Card Number: 76-1423-40
SBN: 8415-2034-8
First Printing
Printed in the United States of America

The McCall Publishing Company
230 Park Avenue
New York, N.Y. 10017

Jones

Jones was the name of a dog named Jones.

And Jones
loved
bones.

Every bone Jones saw around
Jones would bury in the ground
every shape and size of bone
every kind of bone that's known
Jones wanted for his own.

Friends of Jones would telephone,
"Jones, old boy, lend me a bone."

"I don't have a bone to loan,"
groaned Jones.
"I only have the ones I own,"
moaned Jones.

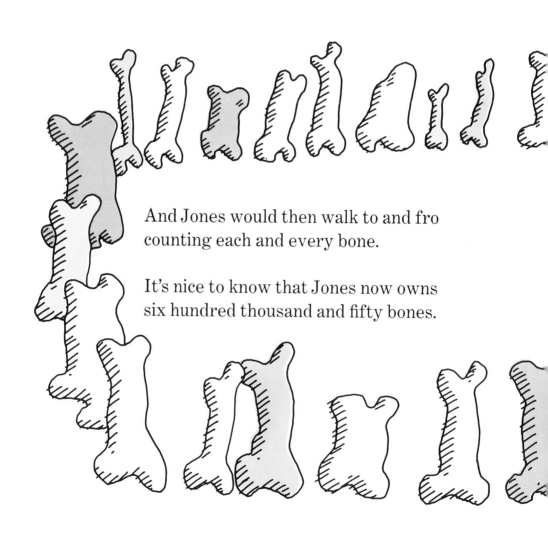

Every other Tuesday Jones
would go to dig up all his bones
and line them all up in a row.

And Jones would then walk to and fro
counting each and every bone.

It's nice to know that Jones now owns
six hundred thousand and fifty bones.

"When I get my millionth bone
I'll be glad to make a loan,"
says Jones
counting once again his bones.

Jones
loves
bones.

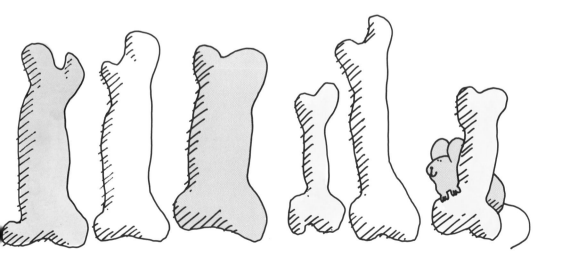

The
Cat
and the
Bat

A cat is a cat

A bat is a bat

A mat is a mat

Now we've had enough of that –
Let's get on with the story.

A cat and a bat sat on a mat.
"Let's chat," said the cat
as he sat with the bat.
"Let's chat about this
and let's chat about that,"
said the cat to the bat
as they sat on the mat.

So they started to chat.

"Do cats like bats?"
said the bat to the cat.

"I don't know," said the cat
"I don't know till I try."

And the cat ate the bat
without batting an eye.

"That's that," said the cat,
"but I'm happy to say
cats do like bats
in the very worst way."

Now the cat sits on the mat.

"I feel fat," says the cat.

And that's that.

Harry

Harry had a hat.
Harry always wore his hat
whether it was cold or hot
whether it was hot or not
Harry always wore his hat.

Harry had a coat.
Harry always wore his coat
whether it was cold or hot
whether it was hot or not
Harry always wore his coat.

Harry had a cat.
The cat had a hat and coat.
The cat wore his coat and hat
whether it was cold or hot
cold or hot, hot or not
the cat wore his coat and hat.

Harry had a goat.
The goat had a coat and hat.
The goat wore his hat and coat
whether it was cold or not
cold or hot, hot or not
the goat wore his hat and coat.

Harry loved his hat and coat,
Harry loved his cat and goat
And Harry also loved his boat.

His cat and goat loved hats and coats
and things like Harry, things like boats.
Harry and the cat and goat
are out there floating in the boat.
Each wears a hat, each wears a coat.

Wave to them out in the boat
To Harry and his cat and goat
And then they might ask you to float
with all of them out in the boat.
(Be sure to wear your hat and coat.)

The Mouse and his Friend

A mouse said something the other day.

I didn't know what to say.

"Something," said the mouse.

I said nothing at all
because
I didn't know what to say.

I am not very good
at carrying the conversational ball.

The mouse brought a friend.

They said something to me, those mice.

They said something once, they said something twice.

"Something, something," they said,
the mouse and his friend.

"Something, something," they said
and that was the end
of my talk with the mice.

The mice, I thought, were very nice.